Robert Tregoning

OUT of the BLUE

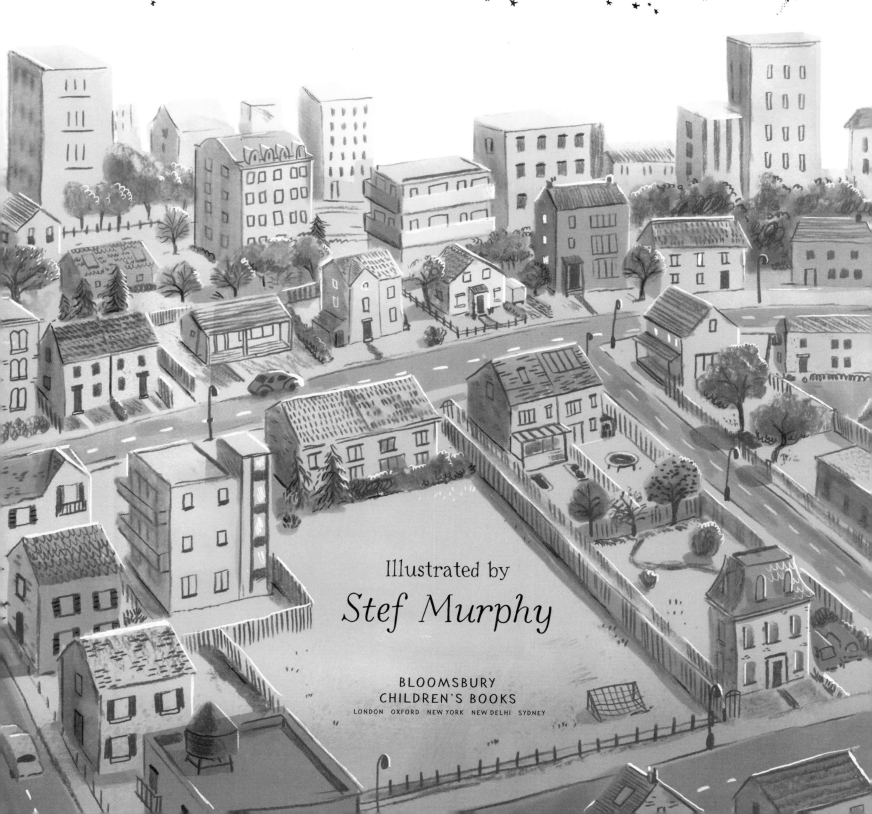

Illustrated by

Stef Murphy

BLOOMSBURY
CHILDREN'S BOOKS
LONDON OXFORD NEW YORK NEW DELHI SYDNEY

In a very BLUE house,
on a very blue street,
in his stripy blue pyjamas
on his blue bed sheet . . .

ONLY BLUE ALLOWED

BY BLUE GOVERNMENT DEMAND.

ANYTHING THAT ISN'T BLUE, BY COLOUR LAW, IS BANNED.

For Billy, because of Billy - R.T.

For Mum and Dad - S.M.

BLOOMSBURY CHILDREN'S BOOKS
Bloomsbury Publishing Plc
50 Bedford Square, London, WC1B 3DP, UK
29 Earlsfort Terrace, Dublin 2, Ireland

BLOOMSBURY, BLOOMSBURY CHILDREN'S BOOKS and the Diana logo are trademarks of Bloomsbury Publishing Plc
First published in Great Britain 2023 by Bloomsbury Publishing Plc

A catalogue record for this book is available from the British Library

ISBN 978 1 5266 2797 1 (HB)
ISBN 978 1 5266 2796 4 (PB)
ISBN 978 1 5266 2795 7 (eBook)

1 3 5 7 9 10 8 6 4 2

Printed and bound in China by Leo Paper Products, Heshan, Guangdong

MIX
Paper from
responsible sources
FSC® C020056

To find out more about our authors and books visit www.bloomsbury.com and sign up for our newsletters

sat a worried little boy
who was feeling very blue.
He loved the colour YELLOW,
but no one else knew.

The boy got dressed that morning
and, as always, made no fuss.

He waved goodbye to Dad
and ran to catch the blue school bus.

He looked out of the window
and he watched the blue world pass.
It made him sad to see the workers
painting trees and grass.

Once at school, he went outside and joined the litter pick.
Anything that wasn't blue was tossed in bin bags quick.

A dump truck came that afternoon, to take what had been found.
And the rainbow-coloured rubbish was buried underground.

This little boy, however,
    lifted something from the truck
and hid inside his bag . . .

a little, YELLOW
rubber duck.

He raced back home to add it to his secret, closet stash
of YELLOW things he'd rescued
from the technicolour trash.

"Dinner's ready," came Dad's call.
It gave the boy a fright!
He hid his yellow duck away
and shut the blue doors tight.

He sat and ate blue cheese on toast
and wished he could tell Dad . . .

But in his heart he felt that
loving YELLOW must be

BAD.

That night in his bedroom,
    while the world was fast asleep,
the boy crept to his closet,
    just to have a little peep.

He lifted out his rubber duck
    and handled it with care.
        Then in a sudden flurry . . .

... tossed his treasures in the air!

All his things flew round the room like dancing YELLOW kites.

His sticky notes,

his submarine,

his pair of yellow tights.

He leapt into the whirling glow
and **bounced** among it all.
But twirling round, he heard the sound . . .

. . . of FOOTSTEPS
in the hall!

He heard them creeping closer
and he stood in total SHOCK.

He saw the landing lights
turn on and heard the . . .

KNOCK,

KNOCK,

KNOCK!

He watched
the handle turn
and heard
the creaking
of the door.

There was
NO time
to tidy up –
his dad
walked in
and saw . . .

. . . YELLOW things crash landed, on the carpet, from the air.
Dad saw his son, stood frozen,
yellow stuff spread everywhere.

The boy was terrified —
he could not breathe, he could not think.
He felt his dad's eyes on him and he felt his stomach sink.

"Don't worry," said Dad softly. "I'm your dad and I love you.
So if you DO love yellow,
then I know just what we'll do."

That wasn't what the boy had thought his dad was going to say.
But Dad's words made him think . . .

Could loving
YELLOW
be OK?

They bounced down
their blue staircase
and through their
blue front porch,

then out into their garden by the light of their blue torch.

The boy watched as Dad searched
inside the back of their blue van,
for everything that they would need to carry out his plan.

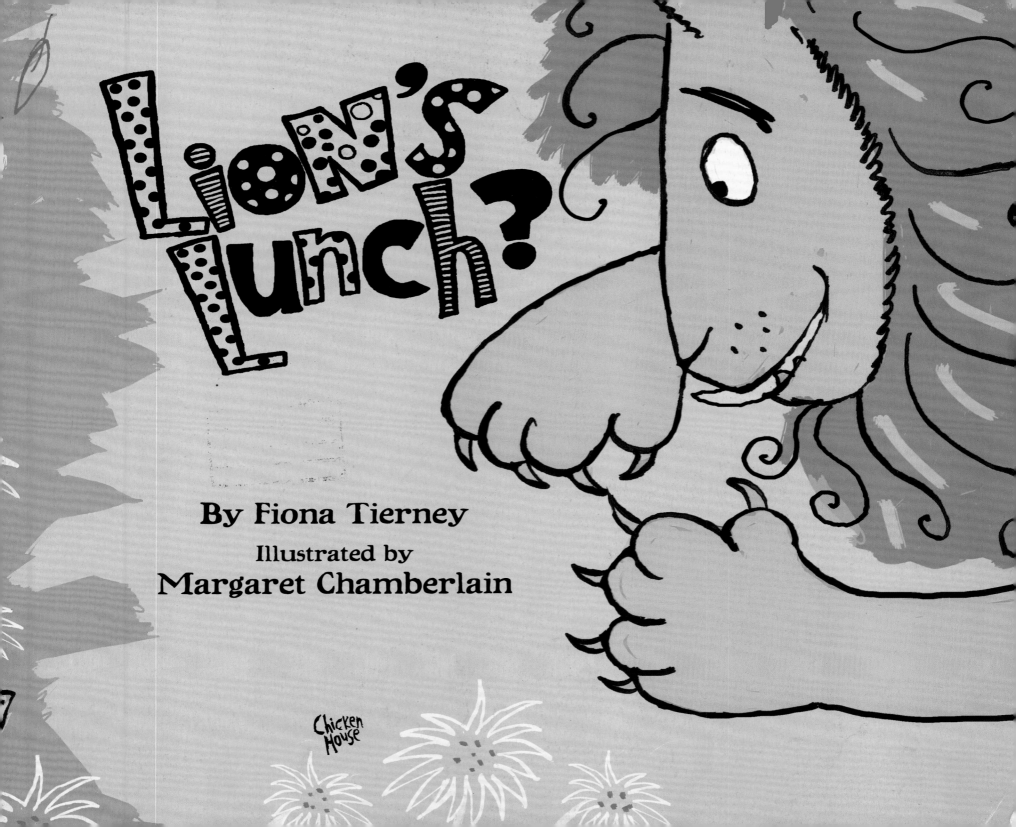

Lion's Lunch?

By Fiona Tierney

Illustrated by
Margaret Chamberlain

Chicken House

Sarah was walking through the jungle singing happily when a big lion pounced from behind a bush.
'**What are you doing in my jungle?**' he roared.

'P-please Mr Lion,' whispered Sarah, 'I was only going for a walk.'

swoop

lumber

prowl

gallop

flit

'A WALK! Nobody here just walks.
We run, sprint, prowl, creep, swing,
lumber, slither, swoop, gallop, flit,
and scuttle. You shouldn't be
here, this is my jungle.'

'I'm sorry, I didn't mean
to bother you,' said Sarah.

'And what was that
sound?' snapped Lion.

'I was s-singing,'
said Sarah.

'SINGING! Nobody here just sings.
We roar, yowl, grunt, chatter,
buzz, trumpet, hiss, growl,
pant and harrumph.'

grunt

oink

hiss

'I'm sorry,' said Sarah.
'I didn't mean
to bother you.'

ROAR

grunt

croak

'Since you shouldn't be here
I'm going to eat you!' said Lion.

'Please don't eat me,'
pleaded Sarah.
'I love the jungle.
Tell me what
I can do to stay.'

'Let me see,' jeered Lion, ticking off his sharp **claws** one by one.

'You can't run like Cheetah,
or climb like Monkey,
or swim like Crocodile,
or stalk like Tiger,
or leap like Gazelle,
or hide like Chameleon,
or reach like Giraffe,
or wallow like Hippopotamus,
or float like Butterfly,
or wriggle like Snake.

Now I'm out of **claws**, and it looks to me like you're LUNCH!'

Lion licked his lips
and got ready to **leap**.

'Wait,' said Sarah.
'If I can do something

that nobody else in the jungle

can do, will you

let me stay?'

'What can you possibly
do that we can't do
better?' asked Lion.

'**I can draw,**'
said Sarah.

'Draw?' said Lion taken aback. 'What can you draw?'

'You,' replied Sarah quickly as she took out her paper, pencils and paints. 'After all – you are the King of the Jungle.'

As she drew, the other jungle animals gathered behind her.

'Finished,' said Sarah at last, and she showed Lion her picture.

Lion looked.
Lion saw . . .

a great big cross lion!

'That's not **me**,' he growled.
'I'm handsome, but you've
made me look angry and mean.
I will eat you because you
can't draw.'

'OH YES SHE CAN!' chorused the other animals. 'You're bad-tempered and bossy. Let her draw us and you'll see.'

So, while Lion sulked, Sarah drew all the other animals.

Friendly Squirrel

'See!' said the animals. 'Sarah can only draw what she finds. It's not her fault you don't like it.'

Lion looked at his picture and at the other drawings. Then he looked at Sarah and the other animals. 'You are right,' he said in a voice that was quiet and thoughtful. 'Sarah, you are free. It's getting late, let me walk you safely out of the jungle.'

'NO,' said the other animals, 'you are too grumpy and bossy. We will go with Sarah.'

And they all set off in a merry, noisy,
happy bunch, with Lion following far behind.

When everybody had said goodbye,
Lion came up to her and said,
'I don't like the way I look.
Sarah, I wish I could change.'

'You are a big, strong and
wonderful lion,' said Sarah.
'Maybe you could try helping
everybody instead of bullying
them. I'm sure that will change
the way you look!'

'Please come back and draw me again.
You'll see a difference, I promise,'
said Lion.

'Of course,' said Sarah,
'I'll come again next month.'

And guess what she drew this time?

A GREAT BIG HAPPY LION!

When she was
finished, Lion smiled.
'Sarah, I was wrong.

You are welcome to walk and sing and draw in OUR jungle whenever you like!'

When asked to do the washing-up,
"YES!" is what he said.

When asked to fetch the firewood,
he would rush off to the shed.

When asked to pick the cabbages,
Ned wouldn't whine or stress.

He *always* answered *straight away*
and always answered . . .

"YES!"

And when, each night, the **dragon** came,
swooping through the sky,
the knights would holler, "Get inside!"
and, "**YES!**" Ned would reply.

This happened each and every night.
The dragon circled down
and frightened all the grown-ups
as she swept around the town.

They'd rush inside their cottages.
"Phew! That was close!" they'd say.

But Ned would watch the dragon
as she slowly flew away.

He thought he heard the dragon sigh
and give a little groan.
Ned wondered, "Is she just like me?
Perhaps she's all alone?"

But then, Ned's parents said, "Goodnight,"
and told him, "Bedtime, Ned."
And what would Ned say? . . .

"YES!" (of course)
and off he'd go to bed.

Until the morning Ned awoke
and something strange occurred.

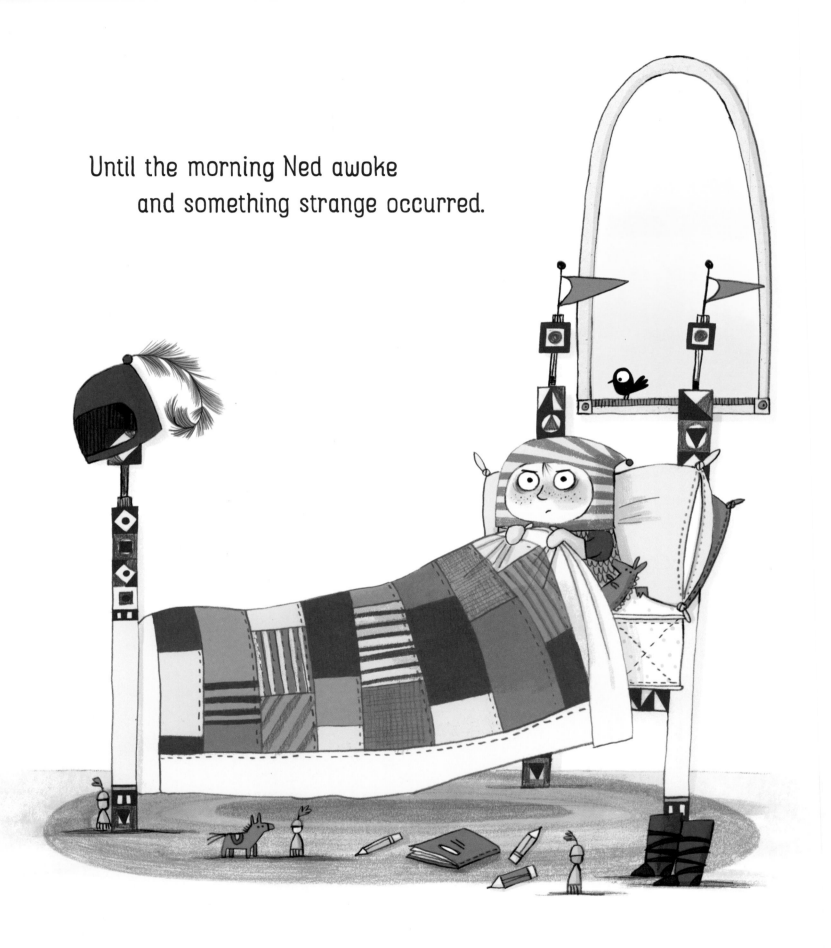

When Mum said, "Son, please fetch the milk!"
Ned found a different word.

He felt quite odd: all hot inside,
and cross from top to toe.
He shook his head from side to side
and then Ned answered . . .

"NO!"

His mum was shocked!
She stood and stared . . .

as Dad came in to say,
"Ah! Will you help me,
Ned, my lad?
The tournament's today.

Now, can you find my shield?" he asked.
"My arrow and my bow?"

But Ned still felt all prickly
and so he answered . . .

"NO!"

Well, that was just the start of it!
The "NO!"s came thick and fast!

"NO!" Ned told the butcher
when he wanted to get past.

"NO!" Ned told the baker
when she wanted Ned to pay.

"NO!" Ned told the fisherman.
"We don't want fish today!"

His parents
couldn't understand.
"What has got into Ned?"
They called him in –
"It's time for tea!" But,

"NO!"

Ned shook his head.

Suddenly, Ned heard a WHOOSH
and saw a flash of light.
The dragon, with her shiny teeth,
came soaring through the night!
The knights all shouted, "GET INSIDE!"
"Quick! Hurry, Ned!" they said.

But Ned clenched up
his fists so tight!
And . . .

"NO!"

yelled Ned.

The dragon circled in the sky,
then landed on the ground.
Hands on hips, Ned waited, but . . .
the dragon made no sound.

So Ned walked slowly up to her
and *poked* her on the toe.
"*You're* supposed to roar!" Ned said.

The dragon whispered . . .

"No . . . I'm so fed up of roaring and I'm rather lonely, too.
     I wonder," sniffed the dragon, "if there's room to stay with you?"
Ned looked quite uncertain and he nearly answered "NO!"
     But when he saw the dragon's tears, his *cross* began to go.

He didn't feel so prickly.
His *angry* was no more.
He felt a little *brighter*,
sort of *lighter*, than before.

Then Ned looked at the dragon
(trying so hard to impress)
and thought,
"There's just one thing to say."
He told the dragon . . .

Then sometimes Ned would hear
a shout of, "BEDTIME!" from below.
And mostly Ned would answer, "YES!"

but sometimes . . .

Ned said, "NO!"

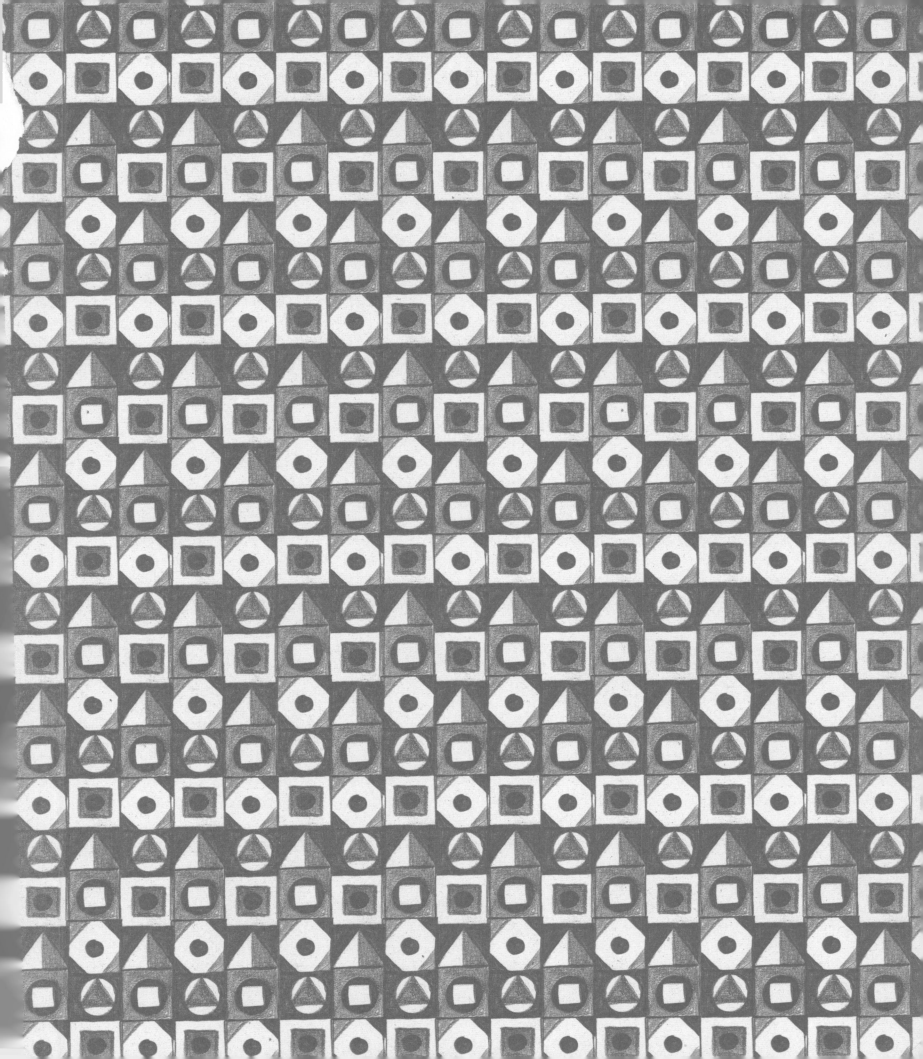

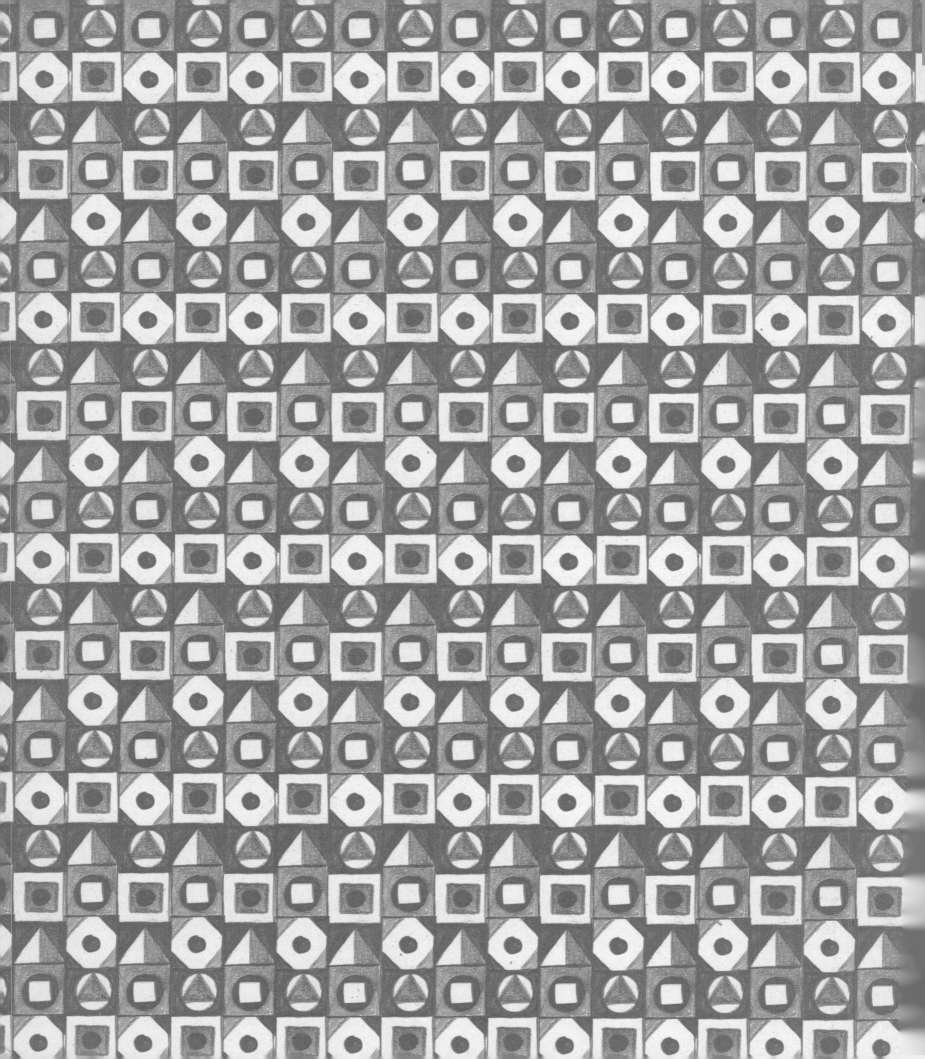